THE GOLDEN GOOSE

by Susan Saunders

pictures by Isadore Seltzer

SCHOLASTIC
HARDCOVER
SCHOLASTIC INC. / *New York*

Library of Congress Cataloging-in-Publication Data
Saunders, Susan
The golden goose.
Summary: Simpleton's generosity helps him
gain a princess for his bride.
[1. Fairy tales. 2. Folklore—Germany]
I. Seltzer, Isadore, ill. II. Title.
PZ8.S265Go 1987   398.2'1'0943 [E]   87-20525
ISBN 0-590-41544-1

12 11 10 9 8 7 6 5 4 3 2 1   1   8 9/8 0 1 2 3/9

Printed in the U.S.A.   23

FIRST SCHOLASTIC PRINTING, JANUARY 1988

To Artemis Millan
—S.S.

To Joyce
— I.S.

LONG AGO, there was a poor woman
with three sons.
The oldest son was tall and handsome.

4

The second son was strong and quick.

The third son was kind.
But he was not handsome.
He was not strong, or quick, either.
His older brothers laughed at him.
They called him names.
"You are nothing but a simpleton!"
they said.
So Simpleton he remained.

One morning, the handsome son went to
the forest to chop wood.
His mother had baked him a honey cake.
She gave him sweet wine to drink while he worked.
The handsome son had not walked far when
he met an old gray man.
"I am so very hungry," the old man cried.
"I am so very thirsty.
Would you give me a bite of your cake?
Would you share your sweet wine?"
"Share my cake and wine?" said the handsome son.
"Then there would not be enough for me.
Out of my way!"
And he turned his back on the old gray man.
But he had hardly begun to chop wood when
his ax slipped!
It cut deeply into his arm!
The handsome son hurried home to his mother.

The next morning, the strong second son left for the forest.
He took with him a honey cake his mother had baked.
She gave him sweet wine to drink as well.
But he had not gone far when he met the old gray man.
The old man asked for a bite of cake and a drop of wine.
But the second son replied, "If I give you any,
I will have less myself.
Away with you – I have work to do!"
The second son had hardly begun to chop
when *his* ax slipped!
He cut his leg so badly that he could
barely limp home.

9

The next morning Simpleton said, "Today *I* will chop the wood."
"Both your brothers have come to harm," said his mother.
"And they are much smarter than you are."
But Simpleton begged, and at last she said yes.
There was nothing sweet for Simpleton, however.
His mother gave him a hard cake, baked in ashes, and
sour, leftover beer.
When he reached the forest, Simpleton met the old gray man.
"I am so hungry and thirsty," the old man said to him.
"Would you share a bit of the sweet cake in your pocket?
Or a drop of your wine?"
"I have only a hard cake baked in ashes, and some sour beer,"
Simpleton replied. "But I will be happy to share with you."
But when Simpleton unwrapped his cake, it was sweet as honey.
The sour beer had turned into the finest wine.
Simpleton and the old man ate and drank their fill.

"You have a good heart," said the old man then.
"I will give you good luck to go with it."
  He pointed to a tree. "Cut down that pine.
  You will find something hidden in its roots."

Simpleton chopped down the pine.

There was a goose nesting among its roots.

And – wonder of wonders! The feathers of the goose were pure gold!

Simpleton picked up the goose.

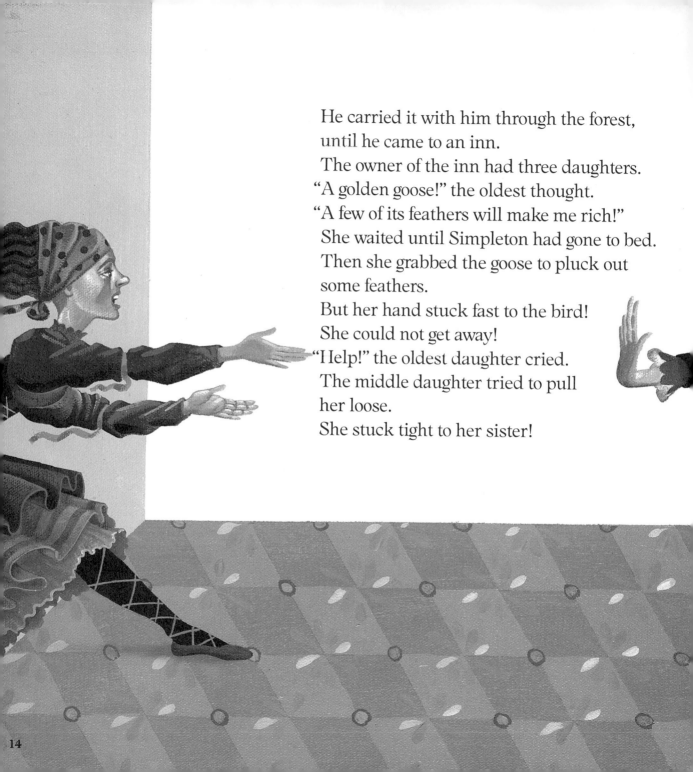

He carried it with him through the forest,
until he came to an inn.

The owner of the inn had three daughters.
"A golden goose!" the oldest thought.
"A few of its feathers will make me rich!"
She waited until Simpleton had gone to bed.
Then she grabbed the goose to pluck out
some feathers.

But her hand stuck fast to the bird!
She could not get away!
"Help!" the oldest daughter cried.
The middle daughter tried to pull
her loose.
She stuck tight to her sister!

"Do not come any closer!" they screamed at the youngest daughter.
It was too late — she was already stuck to the other two.

In the morning, Simpleton picked up the goose and
went on his way.
He paid no mind to the three girls
trailing behind him.
But a parson saw the sisters running to keep up.

"For shame!" he scolded. "You must not run after
a boy like that!"
He tried to drag the youngest sister away.
As soon as he touched her, he stuck fast himself.
Now the parson had to run after Simpleton, too.

Soon they met the sexton.
"Where are you going in such a hurry?" he asked the parson.
He touched the parson's sleeve...and the
sexton was trapped as well.

"Free us!" the sexton called out to two
husky farmers on the road.
It was not long before they were caught as
surely as the others.

Now, the king who ruled the next town
had a daughter, Prunella.
"She will marry the man who can make her lau
said the king.
Prunella was a very gloomy girl.
She rarely smiled and *never* laughed.

21

But when she saw Simpleton…and the golden goose…
and the three sisters…and the parson…
and the sexton…and the two farmers…
the princess laughed until her sides hurt!
"This is the man I will marry," she declared.

But the king was not happy about a
son-in-law named Simpleton.
Prince Simpleton? It simply would not do.

So the king told Simpleton, "You cannot
marry Prunella yet.
First you must find a man who can drink all
the wine in my cellar."
Simpleton was dismayed – the king had a very large cellar.
Then he thought of the old gray man.
"I will ask him to help me," Simpleton said to himself.
He found the old man in the forest, sitting on
the fallen pine tree.
"I am always so thirsty!" cried the old gray man.
"I never have enough to drink!"
Simpleton took him straight to the castle, where the
old gray man drank and drank.
By the end of the day, not a drop of wine was left.

"Now we can marry," Simpleton said to Prunella.

"No," said the king. "First you must find a man who can eat
a whole mountain of bread."
He put every baker in the town to work.
Simpleton called on the old gray man again.
"I am always so hungry," the old man moaned when
he saw Simpleton.
"I never have enough to eat."
"Today you will," said Simpleton.
The old gray man ate the king's bread until not
a crumb was left.

"Now we can marry!" said Prunella.
"No!" said her father. " Simpleton must bring me a ship
that sails both on land and on sea."
"A ship that sails both on land and on sea?"
Was there such a thing? Simpleton shook his head sadly.

He went back to the forest to talk to the old gray man.
"You have a good heart," the old man told him.
"So I have drunk for you, and eaten for you.
 And I will give you the ship."
 The old man tapped the pine tree with his hand.
 It turned into a lovely ship, with tall pine masts
 and silken sails.

Simpleton sailed through the forest, right up to the castle.
The king knew he was beaten.
Simpleton and Prunella were married that very day.
The three sisters, the parson, the sexton,
and the two farmers all came to the wedding.
And so did the golden goose.